AF300626

Impressum

Bibliografische Information der Deutschen Nationalbibliothek: Die Deutsche Nationalbibliothek verzeichnet diese Publikation in der Deutschen Nationalbibliografie; detaillierte bibliografische Daten sind im Internet über dnb.dnb.de abrufbar.

Verlag:
BoD · Books on Demand GmbH, Überseering 33,
22297 Hamburg, bod@bod.de

Druck:
Libri Plureos GmbH, Friedensallee 273,
22763 Hamburg

ISBN: 978-3-8192-4487-2

A Bank Robbery is not the Goal

Opportunities

Observation

Ambition

Basic attitude

Strategy

Information

Tactics and preparation

Risks

Plan and change of plan

Professionalism

Risk and risk mitigation

Luck

The reliable man

Delegation and leadership

Assumptions

Time

Clarity about the goal

II

People usually pay little attention to everyday things. That is what I build on. Only those, who know everything, understand the simple principle of my plan and see through it. That is the danger I live with, but also the thrill of doing it. My thinking revolves around this danger.

Anything that shouldn't be revealed should fit quite inconspicuously into its surroundings. And if there are several things that must remain undiscovered they must not have any obvious connections to each other. But they cannot be completely detached from each other. For what has no connections to each other does not exist together. This is the basic principle of my plan. This plan is like an invention, like a tinkerer I work on it until the plan is perfect. Not perfect for everyone, it is enough if it is perfect for me. Day and night it accompanies me wherever I am. The plan drives me and gives me a feeling of morning dawn.

It was just a moment when it all began. A brief moment, the kind that rarely happens in life. I paused. The atmosphere that surrounded me evoked a memory in me, like in the past, far back, maybe from childhood. A peaceful life opened up to me as my gaze roamed over that bay so picturesque, over the slopes as they rose gently, all the way up, and still green overgrown at the top of the line, where only the wide sky stretches over them. What a beautiful piece of earth, so quiet. The houses had something elegant, modest, each different for itself, and you could see that people were taking care of them. People from all over, and who would ask where I came from, what I did, what my story was. And if so, I would offer them a story that would be simple and consistent in itself. People would not need to know anything more about me, why should they? Yes, this is where I could be, this is where I would arrive. Just how do I get here?

Because my life had not been peaceful. I am well known, almost a little famous, but I have lived unrecognized for so many years now. They call me old Joe, but they have no idea who I am.

It has not been a steady life I have led, but soon that is to change.

For what I am about to undertake is based on a simple consideration: I would fit in well here, despite all I had done, despite my past. Just this one thing - I need three million dollars in cash. With that I could find peace in this beautiful place. It would be other people's money, of course, as I have always held it. Why should I change what has worked.

I have checked my idea several times and it is right for me. Now it has become my goal. All further considerations are derived from it and are driven by criminal energy. It is in my nature, in the nature of a bank robber.

So how do I bring it about? Where could the money come from? It doesn't necessarily have to be a bank robbery, not even for a bank robber. There may be a different way. This different creates new possibilities for me.

Possibilities.

There are always more possibilities than you think. Even if you reinvent the world, there are still more pos-sibilities. Something really new is often not recognized by outsiders at first and therefore easily dismissed. Start right here. It is good if an idea is shadowy to others at

There are many sources of money, but not all of them suit me and my intentions. Banks have always fascinated me because they are proud, tidy and clean. At least until I was there. I know their sluggish and uniform processes well even if they seem almost boring. The fascinating thing for me was always to march through them in a line, open them up and expose their security concept. So precisely that the criminologists knew who had done it. That was my pride, my thrill, the reason to do it again and again. Some banks I cracked just to show how weak they were. A few times I didn't take anything, it already felt like loftiness. How proud I was when the following morning open doors were shown to the public that were previously considered safe. But pride is dangerous because it can make one careless. And carelessness would only have to be my undoing once, then they would have me. If then everything comes out what I've done, I'd be in a place I'll never get out of again. Better not. So be careful, professional, but never proud.

Banks have learned over time, but mostly they defend themselves by hoarding less and less cash. That's not good for me. Another source could be the many business people with cash. And those among them who hold on to cash, at least large sums, are a bit like me - cause they hardly ever ask themselves where the money might come from, but they think a lot about where to put the money. Cash has an appeal for a bank robber, but for its owners it is almost a worry. I help these people. A secrecy surrounds them, and great security gaps open up around these inexperienced ones. I like that. Now there is scent in the air.

> *Observation.*
> *There are big notes and small notes in the market. If you take the time to observe everything and everyone closely, you will find those people with the big notes and understand how they behave and move their money.*

Online transfer businesses would be another option, and there would be many sources in for me, almost the entire financial framework behind the reality of our world. But online is not good. I can cover traces, but digital traces cannot always be completely erased. The systems remember a lot, they can't forget, they can possibly reveal things I hadn't thought of. Systems are not as weak as people - if I exclude a few criminologists, those who are brilliant, who work alone because others can hardly follow them, who never leave a track, and who are similar to me in the end. Danger emanates from them. At some point such a tracker might suddenly appear in front of my door, behind him two men who don't say anything, whom basically he doesn't need either. And he tells me: He knows that I did it, and he knows all the details because he put the pieces of the mosaic together. At that moment everything would be lost for me. He would have found me, even at the end of the world. He and I would know that he is the better one. Smarter, more consistent, more brilliant. I don't want to let it come to this moment. I have to be better before that.

> *Ambition.*
> *I don't know if I 'm going to win, but I know I have the skills. But if there is only one opponent in my profession who is superior to me, I am finished. It is not the fear of failure that holds me back, instead it is the thrill of being the best that drives me.*

In my coups, I have one premise that I unconditionally uphold and will uphold this time as well even if it takes away some sources of money from the start: No guns. I don't kill anyone. I work with my mind, not with a gun. Because if things go wrong, they can accuse me of many things, but not everything.

> *Basic attitude*
> *There are rules and limits. Even for a bank robber. And I will abide by them.*

I have carefully observed what is happening in the world of cash, and have thought a lot about the people who deal with it. With these considerations I decide on my strategy: Private cash in large bank notes is the starting point. Whether legal or illegal, registered or not, it doesn't matter. This cash, collected and gathered by business people, is initially still in private secured rooms. Then comes the point where private individuals hand over their cash in closed cassettes to security guards for transport. A transport possibly to a bank, to a company, for me it is a kind of collection point. The times when money is transported become routine for people. And for the security services the job becomes routine. I look for the weak points in these procedures and pick one. This is where I will go in when the time comes, just very briefly, and the flow of the security guards' routine will come to a halt. I will take the money cassettes and send them on a new path, on my path. The new path of the money is to run through everyday scenes, each of which must appear unsuspicious. The changes from one scenery to the next must be inconspicuous, they must obviously have nothing to do with each other. The vehicle, the appearance, the transport circumstances, they are different in each section, but they seem ordinary and therefore unobtrusive. I only need to keep calm and walk through the individual sections of my escape route, as it were like one among many. Whoever then wants to follow me should follow trails that leads into nowhere. And thus give me time and distance, which soon make me untraceable.

Everyday things are so close to everyone that no one really notices them. The glances and thoughts of possible observers of my actions, of simple passers-by, and above all my pursuers are supposed to get lost in the banal everyday things of a busy world. And even if they can follow me in one scene, their thread of thought should end abruptly, as if torn off. They look around with no idea where I might have gone. The elements of my plan should be like the disordered stones of a mosaic, each individual stone considered interesting and at the same time strange when viewed on its own. Only for me may the mosaic lie together and contain the solution to the riddle. All others may only see stones that tell them nothing.

Strategy.
Alternative strategies can look very different because at the beginning everything is still open in front of us. We have all the freedom, only the goal is fixed. The more we then understand, the more the possible elements of a strategy are organized. At some point our strategy crystallizes.

Since early morning I have been walking slowly through the streets of the city as if it had never been my city, but everything is as if new, as if I am seeing it for the first time. I don't want to miss anything even if it escapes others. So I watch every van, every shop, always looking for clues as to where the source of the money might begin. There are many trickles of money in the countless business houses, and behind their facades it flows together to be pushed on in larger units and at fixed times by supposed professionals, taken away to the few large pools of money. This part of the route leads through the open streets of the city. The interfaces are security services and transport companies, which are often cut according to the same scheme and resemble each other. Day after day I observe them as if I am seeing them for the first time, trying to absorb these procedures with all my senses. Fixed schemes are supposed to provide security and prevent the actors from making mistakes. But uniformity can eventually make people sluggish at some point, inattentive, and then prone to mistakes. Most mistakes are probably not noticed by anyone, not even by those who commit them, and nobody takes advantage of them. Not yet. So I watch these people and their behavior, day after day, no matter how much time it takes. Until I am sure I have found the crucial mistake in the process, know it exactly, and also those who commit it.

How can I be sure that this mistake will also be committed on that day by the drivers of the van when I intervene? Not at all. But I have to decide on an approach. It is to be this van that maybe only I noticed, these people who drive it, and this weakness of theirs which they show. That will be the most dangerous moment. Again and again I mentally go through the steps for that moment, also to find the last possible point at which I can still get out and retreat without harm. Beyond that point, I have to go through with it. When the day comes and I get to that point, my blood will be hot and my mind cool. I know myself well.

It's an old small garage behind a disused veteran petrol station in a back street, for which I pay the rent for six months in advance in cash. In half a year's time, everything will be far in the past, and no one should have set foot in this place for a long time. This little workshop shall not tell anything. It is very quiet in here. The blind glass of the high windows refracts the sunlight so that one can hardly see through it, but the light still fills the room. Over the past few years, a number of tinkerers have tried their hand at old engines here, leaving a lot behind, going away, others coming but not staying. Now I am tinkering here, single-mindedly, as no one before me has done for a long time. The three delivery vans, lined up expectantly next to each other, I bought in various towns in the area, each one selected on the basis of a certain model range to which the van must correspond. The first van is cut like an armored car. Even if it doesn't look like one yet, the old vehicle. The second van is built like one of those many small post office vans. The third is a nondescript white panel van without any blemishes. This one has to cover the longest distance. There is no license plate attached to any of the three, they can be found at short notice. Much more important is the material in the boxes in front of me - paints, wide adhesive foils, a lot of stuff which I had written down on a small list which I now burn in an ashtray. Yes, and I'm waiting for Jack. He wants to be here at four this afternoon.

It's four, and there he is. I had called him in the morning from a café that still has a landline which paying guests are welcome to use. I've worked with Jack a few times before, those were good times, good for us. Now I need a second man, and who that should be and why, I've given that a lot of thought. The good thing about thoughts is that you don't have to share them with anyone. If you have something in mind like I do, you have to go through a lot of thoughts and are only allowed to express very few of them. Jack isn't someone who would ask me why him? He knows why I want him for the job.

We meet here, in the workshop. If I trust someone, it's from the beginning. Even if he says no, we could look at each other with a smile, nod once, and he would walk back out that door without our trust being lost.

So we get straight to the point. I tell him what I'm about. First my goal, then I pause and watch him ponder about why I might have set myself this goal, but more likely if his goals align with mine. His and mine don't necessarily have to be the same; but they have to go hand in hand. What he does with his share of the loot at the end of our journey is entirely up to him. He gets the same share as I do, however high or low the whole may be. That's the deal, and so now he knows how important everything is to me; and he also knows that it will probably be my last coup.

Jack likes my plan. We go over it several times, and his eyes for the details of the sequences, interfaces, and twists I have worked out is as valuable to me as the plan itself. He wants to understand it, asks only a few questions; he doesn't want to change anything. His approval reassures me, and he can see it in my face. The second man, I have chosen the right one.

> *Information*
>
> *Not everyone needs to know everything. But as soon as I take someone into my confidence, he must have full insight into the goal, strategy, and tactics. Only this way can he approve or improve my plan, and my plan becomes his plan.*

We make the same agreement as last time: no mobile phones, no notebooks, nothing digital, we are not allowed to use such equipment or carry them with us. Nothing like that. There is already enough digital stuff out there that can be our undoing. What must not be found should not exist at all. It is easier to stay secret that way. Individual parts of the plan must not have detectable connections to other parts.

And digital is a big danger in my line of work. Mobile phones, surveillance cameras, and their seamless meshing are my adversaries. Tracking is a killer. But old vehicles have no navigation, and that's why I've chosen these vans.

Shortly after sunrise we are back in the workshop and get started. Jack knows exactly what he is doing. The first van is masked off and painted dark. The foils are a lot more work, the colors of the lettering, the emblems, all the details that make our van look confusingly similar to the other one out there. Inside, I check every part to see if it is as you would expect it to be in a cash in transit van from that company. This first car only needs to apparently fulfil what it claims to be, nothing more.

The second will be a mail van, one of the kind you've seen a thousand times before. The procedure is the same - colors, paintwork, details. The foil for the lettering for this and the third car is transparent and held in a wide stripe on which we apply the letters. We stick the foils in one piece on the post van so that we can remove them later just as easily, quickly and in their entirety. No lines or surfaces of different reflections should remain and make it immediately obvious that these are the cars that may have been seen or filmed. If anyone notices them later, we won't be noticed for a long time.

The third van is that of a caterer, as used by a party service, a small van with windows in both rear doors. Simply painted in matt white, the name and slogan on the foils kept very simple, as is the address, which I know does not exist. The license plates will then spontaneously be taken from somewhere on that day and attached here. If we were stopped and asked for the papers, we wouldn't have them with us, they would be with the boss at the company. Or anywhere else. In the caterer's small delivery room, we build in metal shelves, put large, light plastic crates with covers on them, which we tie down, a few bowls and vases, some decorations, things that someone might have ordered for a maybe 70th birthday party, all nice and neat. We have to go a long way with this car that day.

Tactics and preparation
The tactical steps and their preparation take a lot of time and attention, the thing itself then often goes quickly. It is worth the time to mentally go through the process over and over again beforehand - checking details, correcting mistakes, and becoming sure. Anything prepared is no longer a surprise to me.

No traces. The cars must be as if untouched. If they find us, they still have to prove that we did it. That should be difficult for them. We proceed in such a way that we put everything we used, any leftovers, into bags. The tracks in the cars, our fingerprints, everything must disappear. On that day, we will work only with gloves. In the end, there are only the three vans and the rubbish bags. We simply place the latter next to a few containers on the street, where other rubbish is already standing and will be picked up at some point. After that day in the near future, the workshop will be as empty and quiet as before. And if someone comes months later to ask how things are and might go on, no one would be there and hasn't been for a long time. So for this workshop it remains an episode only, for which there would be no reason to talk about or to remember it.

Tomorrow is our day, it's all prepared. Often we have gone through everything in our minds, looked at the details from different angles and checked them out to get a feeling for the entire process. So many things in the mind, but the multitude of details must not dominate the thinking. You can get lost in that. We have to mentally reduce the complexity to see the whole in one: The big sections of our approach, the turning points, and the danger points. Everything means danger, and in what Jack and I are doing, we cannot avoid danger. We must not avoid the risk, because if we wanted to, we should stay in this workshop and unscrew engines. However, our risks can be calculated, so I know where the most dangerous point is: the moment in front of the bank when we have left our car and meet the drivers of the armored car. Fifty-fifty, even a little less, is how our chances stand at that point in front of the bank. If things turn out differently at that moment, if the men behave differently than we expect, or passers-by walk too close to one of the two cars, then I stop without a word, look at Jack, and he knows: we turn back. We would get back into our car and drive away. Then there would be no coup. At such a point only one can decide. Someone has to be in the lead, and that's me, old Joe.

Risks.
Risks are unavoidable when someone dares to do something, but they are calculable. Unlike uncertainty, which is simply breathing down our necks and which

It is early morning, just before dawn. A touch of the sounds of an awakening city penetrates the silence of our workshop. The license plates for the three cars, borrowed the previous night from cars in a long-term car park, are quickly attached. For our third car, the caterer, I picked up several platters of salads, fruit, and several other fine things from a restaurant the night before, as well as two large bouquets of flowers, and arrange everything on the boxes in the individual shelves of the small interior of our van, place the flowers in large vases with some water on the floor and tie them tightly. A fully loaded van, that's what it looks like, and who would dare open the boxes to see what's inside. They are still empty anyway.

The vans have to be put into position. I get into the post van, Jack takes the caterer. We drive them out of the workshop, close the gate and set off with a few minutes time difference. Taking separate routes, we each reach those points where we park the cars. From there we return on foot and meet again after an hour in the workshop. We put on the clothes as security service drivers wear, shirts, jackets, gloves, a few accessories. All of this was easy to get and now with our armored car it gives a unified picture. Now we have to wait until we can start, the time is precisely calculated.

And the time has come. We have driven the armored car out into the yard, locked the workshop in which nothing of us is left behind, so we get in and drive slowly through the streets of the city, heading for the bank. We turn into the busy avenue that runs in front of the wide square that leads across to the bank's high portal.

Both sides of the street are lined with parked cars. And there in front of us it stands, that armored car of the security company, as expected, in the second row next to the parked cars, its hazard lights switched on, with the square to its right. Two cameras are mounted on the buildings to the left along the street, pointed at the wide square and the bank portal. What may be happening to the right of the vans is in the blind spot of the cameras. From his passenger seat, Jack leans close to his door window and can see the security guards standing to the side of their armored car, by the open side door of the car, smoking a cigarette and looking at the wide square. How can they be so careless, behaving against all rules and instructions. There is a lurking calm in Jack's gaze. Only a hundred meters to drive, we are approaching slowly, stopping right behind that van, car to car, and I switch off the engine.

It begins.

We look at each other, wordlessly, amicably, and then both get out on the right via the passenger door. Now it has to go down as staged. Jack has already opened the sliding side door of our car. We look into the hold of our car, but not to the side, only out of the corner of my eye do I see them standing there. From the small box in the front of our hold I take the bottle with the knockout drops and soak two cotton balls wrapped in gauze bandages with it. Two large plastic boxes, each nearly a meter long and encased in a metal collar, with a firm handle at the top and at each end, are at the ready. I lift one of them with my right hand and take a cotton ball with my left. Jack takes the other box and the second cotton ball. Thus equipped, we look like two security guards on duty, working for the same company as the two men on the car in front of us. We turn to the square, prepare to walk toward the large entrance area of the bank, and exchange a few meaningless words. But I stop, turn to the two men who have been looking questioningly at us, standing there beside their van and between the parked cars, and pause like that for a moment. Jack beside me, apparently continuing our conversation. I walk towards the men - 'Have you been around long?` I ask, and with a reproachful look I add 'standing around smoking, that's forbidden'. The two of them look at each other puzzled and quickly stub out their cigarettes, then, somewhat embarrassed and as if caught, assume their postures. I have approached the half-open sliding door of their van and turn my stern gaze away from them both and over to the open door and into the hold. I look in, here, there, examining, as if this is a check into which the two have unexpectedly found themselves. The first of the two comes assiduously to me and, standing next to me, he also looks into the half-filled hold, which seems dark and disorganized. He starts to say something as if he wants to explain himself. I wait a moment, put my box on the floor and step into the hold, shaking my head. As a security guard, he should never have allowed this, how could he. He lost control of the overall situation. And what does he do? He follows me into the hold. Now. With the numbing cotton ball pressed on his nose with my left hand and my right arm gripping him tightly, it only takes a second - and he collapses. I let him slide slowly to the floor and pull him further back into the hold. Jack had maneuvered himself in front of the door and mumbles something like 'Let them do it, we have to move on'. The second man, irritated by the situation and throwing all the rules of the security service overboard, comes near and looks into the hold as well. Jack is very quick - pressing the cotton ball with the drops into the man's face, Jack grabs him and pushes him straight into the hold where the man sinks to the ground, partly stumbling and struggling for a moment longer. While he's still falling, I grab the man by his jacket and pull him further back. Has anyone seen it here between the cars? Has anyone noticed? That's the risk we couldn't mitigate any further. So we believe. Jack, as agreed, remains on the outside of the car, right by the open door, and looks in at me, almost motionless, all senses focused on the road and the wide plaza behind him. We are waiting. Only for a short time, standing very still in the noise of the city, but long enough as it would take someone who saw something and might come to us - whatever he or she might say or do. Maybe if everything is ok? - Yes, it is. But no one comes. Jack takes a deep breath of relief, steps back half a step, and turns to his right - there is a third man standing directly in front of him. Rather - a woman, in a security guard's uniform. Where is she coming from? From the driver's cabin? Standing there out of nowhere, smiling at him with an expression on her face as if expecting an explanation. 'I'm Susan.' Completely perplexed, Jack turns away to the open door, takes a moment to regain his coolness, sees the cotton ball lying on the floor of the hold, takes it, waits until he imagines the woman's face beside him, and grabs her - as he did the man before. When he feels her resistance give way, he pulls her into the car with him. Dumbfounded, I look at Jack, who still has the shock written all over his face as he lays the woman on the ground. He raises a hand briefly as if to say 'I don't know. She was just there.'

Plan and change of plan.

We plan everything - except for what we don't think about, what we overlook, or what chance throws at us. And yet we plan in every detail. Only in this way can we reduce complexity. In the execution of our plan, a change of plan may become necessary at the very first moment, but this is not proof of an inadequate plan. The constant willingness to change the plan is part of planning. Planning doesn't stop before something is completely finished.

There were three of them, not two. For whatever reason, or from wherever. How can something like that happen? It can. We had approached the armored car from behind and assumed we knew the situation. I had checked everything beforehand, but not today. I wonder if anyone has seen this now. Jack stands next to the van as before, waiting, but nothing happens around him, no one is coming. We shouldn't wait too long. I tie all three of them up and take away their access cards for the doors to the bank's security rooms, which they have access to for transporting valuables. Now - which are the real cash boxes? - here it needs the old Joe. I check every box in the hold, for appearance, weight, texture, the sound when you shake it or turn it, and I know what I'm looking for and how to find it. The cash boxes are often stowed in other containers, but their sound when you move them or they bump against each other is always the same. Anything I scent containing cash boxes I put at the front to the side of the door, and Jack stows the containers in the large dark plastic box I was carrying. These are the only ones we take, nothing else. I get out of the hold, we each grab the box by the handle at its ends and set it down on the road. Once more my gaze passes over the three people in the hold, then I close the side door. Jack switches on the car's ignition and ventilation in the driver's cabin and opens the windows on the driver and passenger side. It mustn't end badly for these three.

> *Professionalism.*
> *I must be able to rely on myself. Know what I have done and know what I have to do. That goes for everyone on the team. Only then can I rely on others.*

Now continue. The box with the cassettes isn't that heavy, we lift it, each on one side, and Jack carries the second box with his other hand, which he also had with him at the beginning. This box contains the postal workers' clothes. So off we stride, as if we do it every day, the few steps across the wide, open square to the high portal of the bank. It is the plain door on the side of the portal intended for the security services, at the corner of the building, which sets back here by two meters. A camera monitors this area, it is pointed at the door, and we cannot avoid it. As soon as we are in its angle of view, we move sideways with our backs to the camera. The access cards work, the door's lock pops open, and we go inside.

I didn't know what it looks like in here. But I have seen a room like this several times during the many years I have been in quite a few rooms where no one wanted me. The room is almost empty, it is only for depositing cash boxes

28

and valuables, which are placed in a lock that closes at the push of a button and does not open again until you have left the room. The bank usually takes over from there. Today it's different. We don't put anything in the lock at all, but close it empty. Instead, we open Jack's second box with the shirts, jackets, and gloves like postal workers wear, change our clothes for these, and put the worn clothes in there. Nothing of ours should be left behind. Less than two minutes later we open the front door again and go out with the two boxes as we had gone in, but this time keeping immediately to the side of the bank, and in five steps we are on the sidewalk. People come towards us without taking any notice of us. Once we have crossed the road, we have to walk a little further before a road turns into it on the right, which I had already seen early this morning. There it is, our little mail van. So we put the two boxes in the hold and drive off, setting course for the second turning point of our act.

I drive calmly and steadily. And the drive does us good, it gives us a few minutes to calm down and the tension eases a little. Police cars come towards us. But the stupor of the three people in their van should still last, it should still be quiet there. And if no commotion has started from the van yet, the square in front of it should also still be quiet, unknowing and unaware for another five to ten minutes. Time is so important. Time means distance to what is happening, distance to possible pursuers.

There on the right is the multi-story car park, that's where our path leads, up the small ramp, opening the barrier with the first of the two day-tickets Jack had bought in the morning, and then the many loops to the fifth upper deck where are hardly any cars at this time. This morning it must have been completely empty when Jack drove up here. Such a beautiful catering van is standing there waiting for us. What party it might go to today? - Now a post van is parked next to it, one parking bay apart. When we open the caterer's van, we notice the smell of the salad platters and the many small delicacies that fills the whole car. The flowers in their water have remained fresh. On the shelves are two white jackets with double rows of buttons, like chefs wear, and which we now change for ours. All buttons closed to the top, and equipped with light-colored gloves and small caps, we henceforth belong to the delivery service of a restaurant. We put our mail jackets and gloves in the box with the other clothes. We grab the ends of the wide foils with the lettering and symbols of the post office and slowly pull them off the vehicle in one piece. After these few days, they peel off the van's paintwork quite easily, and nothing visible remains on the car. With the license plates removed, the post van no longer has a name, bears no clue to what has happened except its color. But you have to know this clue because otherwise there will probably be a car parked here for several days, maybe weeks, that no one will be able to identify. The foil also stowed in the box, we carry both boxes into the caterer and push them into the two remaining open shelves near the floor. On each we drape a long salad bowl. The post van is locked, the key dropped into the gutter drain, so we hop in our caterer and head down the meanders to the exit. The barrier opens with the second card and we whirr down to the road where we drive slowly and mindfully with our precious cargo.

How to reduce risk, that is one of the vital questions in my profession. Passers-by may still have seen and later report how two postal workers put boxes into a car and drove away. This was no longer within sight of the crime because of the blocks of houses, but it was hardly more than a hundred meters distance from the bank. Someone could easily be found who would feel called to report such a detail. This interface may not remain undiscovered for long. Soon enough, the cameras will reveal that while security guards went in through that bank door, postal workers came out. If witnesses do not describe this beforehand. The question of where the two men went, who saw them, will then probably be answered within a short time. Then they look for the post van, but there are many of them. At some point they will have found all the post vans in the area and questioned their drivers. That takes a little longer, but in the end it's only a matter of time. The nameless van in the parking garage may not be questioned until late; its drivers hopefully never.

It is not initially apparent that the mail van and the caterer had any points of contact, and it is highly unlikely that this will be revealed. The parking garage's cameras saw a caterer drive in and drive out again a few hours later. And a mail van drove in. What it doesn't normally do, not in a parking garage. Because what does it want there? When did the post van leave again? Not at all. But it is still not obvious that there is an interface between the post van and the caterer who drives out a good five minutes later than the post van comes in, there is too much movement on the driveway to the parking garage for that. The interface should be practically invisible. Here it is again, the basic idea of my plan. This is the reason why we switched cars.

> *Risk and risk reduction*
> *Dare and risk go hand in hand. We can grasp risks, look at them, and assess them. If the risk is higher than what we want to achieve, we'd better not leave the workshop at first, but work on dismantling and reducing the risk. After that we can take off.*

As we drive away from what we've done, the roads slowly become calmer and a little quieter, and despite turning and changing direction several times, we still head south-west, where after almost half an hour we reach one of the major arterial roads, which we follow for a long time. The city is now behind us. We have gained distance, but we are still the same, with goods in our luggage, the contents of which we do not yet know, but which would provide all the evidence against us. If we were to be stopped and searched now, we could be busted right away, and already tonight the news would say that the case was solved. Yes, and there, far ahead of us in this almost treeless landscape, in a side path, is a car whose color Jack and I don't like. As if lurking, motionless, as if waiting for us. To turn off here would only arouse suspicion. There is hardly any opportunity in this vastness anyway and even less reason for us as caterers to turn off anywhere. The driver of that car has probably chosen his position accordingly. It is inevitable, we drive towards it. Soon we are so close that the driver's contours become clear. We just drive straight on past the police car at a steady speed. Jack sees out of the corner of his eye that the policeman's gaze is following our car. And so it is these two seconds that it usually takes before we see in the rear-view mirror how the police car at first starts to move ponderously, swings into the road in our direction, accelerates rapidly and follows us. It's only a moment, then it's there, staying behind us at only a short distance and keeping our speed. What do we expect now - to hear the siren wail once? The police car pulls to the left into the on-coming lane, accelerates until it catches up with us, stays level for a moment, accelerates again, passes us and moves into our lane in front of us. There he drives as if the two vehicles belong to each other. But they definitely don't. Now he's accelerating - which I hardly have expected any-more. The gap widens and soon he is just a dark dot far ahead of us on the road. You have to be lucky sometimes, with all the planning.

> *Luck*
> *Everything is prepared. Why shouldn't it succeed now?*
> *We have to believe in it.*

We can't feel safe, and it probably always will be that way. Should we get away with it and remain in hiding and undetected for years, for all the time that may come for us, any feeling of security would be nothing but a fallacy. Once you have started out like us, you have to live your whole life according to it until your last day, and even in death remain undetected in order to protect your friends. When I started to live my life the way I have been doing it for decades now, I did not realize what consequences my actions would have for my entire life. If I had started a different life instead, I would not have known the consequences either, but they would probably not be so relentless.

We are almost two hours on the road, and now there, far back in the field, a small dwelling with a barn becomes visible. The house is only occupied by migrant workers at harvest time, a very simple house, and many months of the year it stands empty, as it does at this time. There will be no family celebration there today, and yet a caterer is now heading towards it. We roll across the small courtyard, past the house, and stop in front of the barn. It's more of a shed, very high but with a solid cement floor, tidy and maintained, and some harvesting equipment lined up but dusted. This place doesn't seem like one that has been abandoned by its inhabitants, and in a while people will come back here. Maybe just the workers, but possibly the owner, and there will probably be some among them who will organize and divide up what work needs to be done here. Of course, if a van is parked and then covered in dust, these people will immediately notice it and look into it, but I think only up to a certain extent. Then they will give up on not being able to find the driver or the owner of the car and go back to their work. The parked car could become an anecdote that would fade over time and not be told again.

I take a closer look at the buildings to make sure we don't get a surprise - all abandoned. My gaze goes over the vast land all around. Everything is as it should be.

We drive the car into the barn and act as before in the car park: the two boxes are taken out of the car, one with our used clothes, the other with the value inside, around which everything revolves. Again, we pull the foils off the car, fold them up and put them in the box with the clothes, along with the caterer's license plates. We stack the plates with the salads on top of each other and carry them out into the field, where we scatter the salads and everything else on them in the field and clean the plates neatly with paper towels. When the plates are carried back to the wagon, the flowers do the same. As if everything had been prepared like a feast for the field mice.

And there, 100 meters back, it stands, a small Cessna machine, on the wide, firm path that leads from here far into the fields. Just as I expected, and as an old friend had promised me. A feeling of freedom opens up in me. When you do something like this, you need people you can rely on. My friend had flown all his life, including as a bush pilot, on three continents, and he had almost always taken off safely and landed safely. There were people who called him a daring pilot, and he probably was. But this was not without consequences. Once he had come down hard, and he knew when it's good, when to stop. Since then, other people have been flying for him. I told him I needed a reliable man. You will get, he replied. So Jack and I walk towards the plane, and halfway there we see the door open. The pilot has been waiting in the machine, looking at what is going to happen here and who is coming to this remote place. This is smart because there is no reason for a pilot to leave his machine before the people or cargo he is supposed to pick up have actually arrived. He gets out, and in his overalls he looks like a member of the air force. As we get closer, we realize:

the reliable man is a woman. She stands under the wing of her machine and looks towards us, waits at first, and then calmly walks towards us. This is how we face each other. From now on there are three of us. She watches my face, looks over at Jack. And I say 'I'm Joe'. She smiles almost imperceptibly - who else should I be? 'You know how it's supposed to go?' I ask. 'Two people,' she replies. I could ask some questions now, but she doesn't give me the impression as if she had landed her plane here to give answers. She was sent as the reliable man, and I guess she is. Questions and answers would be inappropriate here because she is the pilot who was sent to us, whereas I am not a pilot. I rely on her, and have done since I left the workshop this morning.

> *The reliable man.*
> *It doesn't take a lot of people to implement a plan; it takes the individual, the one who is the right one; people who are sure doing their job. That's where we start. The team is then the result, not the beginning. Because if something gets dicey, I can only get through it with re-liable people.*

'Are you ready?' she asks. - 'Two more boxes,' I reply, 'that's all.' So we turn back to the barn, a few things left to do. It is important to look in every nook and cranny of the van so that nothing is left behind that could indicate us or provide evidence against us. Shelves, boxes, trays, vases, we leave it as it is. Just empty and meaningless. We lower the windows of the car a little so that dust can get in; and I let the air of the tire at the front of the driver's side escape via the valve. None of this means anything when the car is found and looked at, but that's what it is - a broken-down, dusty car that gives no answers.

It is only the two boxes that we take with us as we leave the barn, carefully close the gate again and walk back to the plane. She has been waiting in the shadow of the wing and now opens the double-leaf door of the plane. Both boxes are stowed behind the second bench seat and the rear door is closed. 'Let's take off then,' she says, and we climb into the machine. She closes the door, gets in the front, puts on her headset, and starts the engine. Jack looks to me, and the look on his face tells me he's thinking the same way I am - there are three of us now, and from here on she controls the action. This juncture in our plan feels different to Jack and myself than the previous ones, because before we had everything in our hands, every decision and every moment, and now we are handing this over. That's good because that's the plan, and that's how we execute it. The engine gets louder, she looks around at us for agreement, and we nod at her. The machine moves, accelerates, takes off, gains quickly altitude, and takes a course in a wide arc towards the south. It's 12:10 p.m., the sun is high in front of us, I can see it by the equal shadows of the wing supports on either side. The course is correct and we are well on time.

Delegation and leadership.
I am not a pilot and will not tell a pilot how to fly an aircraft. She knows, and I rely on her. My guidance is as modest as to tell her when and where to fly me.

The land lies far below us, slowly and steadily we pass over it. The colors of the mostly dry earth give an idea of how hot it is down there. Fields and plantations that are irrigated stand out from their surroundings with clear straight lines. This is how it stretches to the horizon. The glaring sun shines on our plane, reflecting in the metal surrounds of the windscreen; there can hardly be a brighter day than up here. In silence we hear the loud whirring of the engine, see the gray shimmering of the propeller, follow our thoughts, reflect on how everything went, look ahead, into the distance and also into our personal time that is to come.

The border between the two countries cannot be made out from up here. I wouldn't have seen it, but the pilot turns to us and points downwards. Then it is probably here, where we leave our country, quite imperceptibly. Basically, it's like all the transitions we've been through today: The change from one to the other is hardly noticeable, almost no traces, we leave behind what has been. We only take ourselves with us, and with us all the past that we carry within us and cannot discard. So what is all this for? It's the appeal of the new thing, the idea of landing the super-coup, committing an almost perfect crime, and honing the perfection. I'd probably do it again and again for that. But it should be the last time, I have firmly resolved that. And I can discipline myself, that's what I've learned, otherwise I wouldn't be here.

Little has changed in the landscape deep below us, it has only become a little more rugged, and above the hills and mountains the wind rises in different currents, making the machine a little restless. Glancing towards us, the pilot draws our attention to a valley stretching to the west and points with a nod to what little is visible down there. Three tiny-looking buildings, their metal roofs glistening in the sun, and the long light grey strip in front of them is then probably the runway. She swings the plane in and begins the descent. The relief of the mountain slopes becomes clearer, everything down there seems deserted, not a car can be seen at the buildings, not a person, nothing moves. The runway is used for the take-offs and landings of the crop-spray planes, during the season the agricultural flights turn this outpost into a busy airfield. But at this time of year, it is very quiet here. During the landing approach, the aircraft rocks a little, then it lies very still and we touch down. We raise a long cloud of dust, which the wind drives into the mountains, where it soon disappears. The pilot does not even turn the plane towards the middle building in front of which we come to a stop, but turns the plane straight back towards the runway. She will not stay here for long. The engine switched off, she takes off her headset and unfastens her seat belt. We hear the silence. She gets out, opens our door from the outside, and so we do the same. We don't need to stay here any longer than necessary either. With the two boxes we go to the middle of the three small halls, whose door is not locked, and set both boxes down on one of the tables. She enters the mostly empty room last and at some distance, keeps to the side and leans against a small cupboard, waiting to see how we would now fulfil our part of the deal. We, on the other hand, do not wait because we have already been waiting a long time. Now we want to see how it turns out, what value we are carrying here, whether it was worth it, whether we succeeded in the coup. It's up to me to open the box with the cassettes. I take out one cassette after the other and place them next to each other on the long table. The last thing I take out is a drill and a cable, all prepared. I know the locking mechanism of this type of cassette very well and drill into three points of the cassette. There are twenty-eight cassettes, but opening the first one seems like a harbinger of what the others may or may not have in store for us. With both hands I lift the lid.

Silence.

They lie tightly packed in four stacks next to each other. Hundred-dollar notes, next to them hundred-dollar notes, then fifty-dollar notes, then hundred-dollar notes again. The lid of the cassette still has the notes pressed together. It is in front of us, our prey. I take out the stacks and place them in front of the cassette, in the same order. Each stack has a distinct weight, which you don't expect when you only have a few notes in your hand. I take the first pile in my hand again, run the thumb of my other hand along the side of the pile, like a card game. Yes, they must all be hundred-dollar notes. They smell like old money. No new notes. I can guess how many notes there are, a stack. Jack just watches, so does she, doesn't even come over to the table. So I open the second cassette, take out what's in it, following the same pattern as with the first. Cassette by cassette. All twenty-eight of them. I did the math, only a rough estimate, but I know how much it is at least. More than we expected, considerably more. Big notes, my calculation worked out. They were people who intended in advance to pay cash, for whatever. No small notes. It must have been large sums that were paid here. Where might the money have come from? Simply private individuals, or are they organized people. Who would I be dealing with if they came after me? The armored car is from a company where all freight is insured high enough. Unless the contents of the cargo are not specified, then the risk for the exact contents remains with the owner. Well, someone will be interested in the whereabouts of the money, and maybe insurance will cover the loss, maybe not. There are always unknowns involved, there is no certainty, not for me. That's just the way it is.

Assumptions

We build strategy and tactics on assumptions. One has to be careful with assumptions because we don't know if an assumption will turn out to be wrong, but one wrong assumption can be a killer. And it only takes one killer to make any success impossible from the start. Three million dollars in cash for each Jack and myself, all in a box carried by the two of us, then it must be big notes. So we assumed, according to the sources of the money, and we were right. Our assumption that there were only two drivers in the armored car was wrong. Susan was unprofessional, which was our good fortune. Assumptions are more than just scraps of paper that fall off the table during planning, don't quite fit into the flow and are therefore declared as an assumption.

The deal is: the flight costs one hundred thousand dollars. Should the total value be less than three hundred thousand, it would be a third of the value. So she gets a hundred thousand. 'In hundreds, I suppose?' I ask. She nods and approaches. So I pull out a couple of stacks from the row, take one, untie the ribbon, and count ten notes on top of each other and then with a slight offset ten again, I count up to ten thousand. Then I leave a hand's breadth free. It goes on like this until the hundred thousand are full. Pushing the sections of ten thousand together, a ribbon around each stack, there they lie, ten bundles, her share. She has a leather bag with her, the ten inside, she closes it, and now she smiles once. The job was worth it, and apparently she could trust us. Just like we trusted her. She turns to the door and goes back to her machine. We look after her, see through the window how she gets on, routinely gets everything ready for take-off, starts the engine and after a few moments is on the runway. There she is already rising, and as naturally as she landed here, she disappears again on the horizon.

From the stacks of money I quickly form two long rows side by side on the table, evenly distributed by eye. It is up to Jack to choose one of them for himself. He chooses none, but sees the one on his side of the table as his as if I have assigned it to him. So the other one is mine. We each quickly put the money back into the cassettes and seal them with tape. That's how it's divided up. Good. Now we have to keep a cool head and not make a fatal mistake on the last stage. When I had spent some time in this area several months ago and had noticed the very bay where the fascinating idea for all this had come to me, I had already thought the whole thing through to the point where I would have to come back on a small plane, quickly, and without border controls. At the time, I had come here with my car to park it and leave it here, just in the back corner of the middle hall, put the license plates in the locked trunk and covered the car with a tarpaulin. That day there was someone at the front of the office who seemed to me to be scheduling the operations here, and I had asked him if I could leave the old car there for a while, for three hundred dollars, it was a lover's model. 'Yes, why not.' More was not asked and not said. When you pave your way with cash, you quickly learn who to ask, when, and for what. There is now some dust on the tarpaulin, but underneath the car is untouched. The engine starts as usual and I drive it out in front of the entrance to the hall. In the trunk there are still the license plates, which I put back on, and also some large empty bags, including a duffel bag; Jack takes this and stacks his cash boxes in it. I spread my cassettes among a few bags and everything is simply stowed in the trunk. Leaving nothing behind, the two plastic crates, all the contents, even our white caterer jackets, we take everything with us on our last stage together.

As we drive away from this remote place, this airfield lying lonely in the middle of nowhere, we talk little, and not about where we are going or what we are about to do now. That is part of our agreement: from now on, we each go our own way, now our paths must no longer cross. It is a long drive to the town where I am to take Jack. He directs me through the streets and where to drop him off. What he has in mind I don't know, but we both know how to behave, especially during the first year that is coming. Above all, we must not make contact with each other. Later it will be possible again, and we also know how we could reach each other should that ever be necessary. Time plays for us, but a coup of this magnitude is not forgotten, and even years later a single carelessness can be fatal for both of us. A life of constant caution is the price we pay.

Jack gets out, picks up his duffel bag, and with a smile he nods to me once more before leaving. I silently wish him good luck.

As I drive through seemingly deserted countryside, I have time to think. From previously three people back to two and now alone again for me. It feels good, this being alone. Nevertheless, I feel responsible for Jack, but not for the pilot. It makes a difference whether you work with friends you take into your confidence or with people in the team who are professionals but remain strangers to you.

As I drive through a small town after a few hours, there are some rubbish containers on the road in front of a school. Here I stop briefly, take all the foils, clothes and whatever else we had used, bundle it up and put it in one of the containers, way down, and drag other rubbish over it. Chance might discover it, but it would still be rubbish to begin with, and the connection to our act is wafer-thin and only exists until the container is emptied in the coming days. Such thin connection threads are unavoidable, but time will soon tear them apart.

A day later I am back where it all began. From up here, I look at the houses down by the water and up the slope, illuminated by the midday sun. Truly, what a picturesque bay. I am at the goal.

The goal was never a bank robbery. What do I want at a bank? There is only danger. My goal is to arrive at this so beautiful place and live here my way.

Would I have achieved this even as a manager? After all, I know what matters. And perhaps that would have been the better way.

<u>Rey-Joe.com</u>